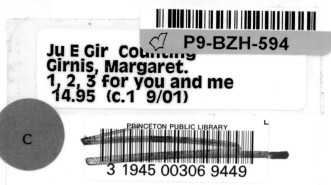

1 2 3

for You and Me

WRITTEN BY **Meg Girnis**

PHOTOGRAPHY BY **Shirley Leamon Green**

Albert Whitman & Company

Morton Grove, Illinois

Also by Meg Girnis and Shirley Leamon Green

A B C for You and Me

Library of Congress Cataloging-in-Publication Data

Girnis, Margaret.

1, 2, 3 for you and me / by Meg Girnis; photographs by Shirley Leamon Green.

p. cm.

ISBN 0-8075-6107-X (hardcover)

1. Counting — Juvenile literature. 2. Down syndrome — Juvenile literature.

[1. Counting. 2. Down syndrome.] I. Title: One, two, three for you and me.

II. Green, Shirley L., ill. III. Title.

QA113.G57 2001

628.9'25 — dc21

00-010258

Published in 2001 by Albert Whitman & Company,

6340 Oakton Street, Morton Grove, Illinois 60053-2723.

Published simultaneously in Canada by General Publishing,

Limited, Toronto.

Printed in the United States of America.

10 9 8 7 6 5 4 3 2 1

The design is by Scott Piehl.

With thanks to God, this book is dedicated to my daughters,
Amanda and Jaimie. Thanks for being in the book
and for being such awesome kids! —M. G.

(Amanda and Jaimie can be seen with the ducklings;
Amanda is also on the cover and with the balloons.)

To all the wonderful boys and girls who helped
make this book a success. —S. L. G.

Meg Girnis and Shirley Leamon Green would like to thank
the Bottego, Burns-Sindon, Colone, Ferner, Ferro,
Hampton-Canady, Hine, Kennis, Linder, Priest, Raptis,
Wesko, and Zelesnikar families for taking time to have
their children photographed for this book.

1

One

Bird

2

Two

Butterflies

Three

Bananas

Four

Dogs

Five

Candles

6

Six

Baskets

Seven

Ducklings

Eight

Books

9

Nine

Boats

Ten

Teddy bears

Eleven

Cars

Twelve

Balls

Thirteen

Shells

Fourteen

Presents

Fifteen

Blocks

Sixteen

Apples

Seventeen

Stars

18 Eighteen

Shoes

19

Nineteen

Hats

Twenty

20

Balloons

1 •

2 • •

3 • • •

4 • • • •

5 • • • • •

6 • • • • • •

7 • • • • • • •

8 • • • • • • • •

9 • • • • • • • • •

10 • • • • • • • • • •

11 • • • • • • • • • • •

12 • • • • • • • • • • • •

13 • • • • • • • • • • • • •

14 • • • • • • • • • • • • • •

15 • • • • • • • • • • • • • • •

16 • • • • • • • • • • • • • • • •

17 • • • • • • • • • • • • • • • • •

18 • • • • • • • • • • • • • • • • • •

19 • • • • • • • • • • • • • • • • • • •

20 •